Ellie McDoodle

HAVE PEN, WILL TRAVEL

Ellie McDoodle

HAVE PEN, WILL TRAVEL

WRITTEN AND ILLUSTRATED BY

Ruth McNally Barshaw

BLOOMSBURY
CHILDREN'S
BOOKS

Dedicated to those who bring
imagination to life.

Published by Bloomsbury U.S.A. Children's Books
175 Fifth Avenue, New York, NY 10010
Distributed to the trade by Holtzbrinck Publishers

Library of Congress Cataloging-in-Publication Data
Barshaw, Ruth McNally.
Ellie McDoodle: have pen, will travel / by Ruth McNally Barshaw.—1st U.S. ed.
p.   cm.
Summary: Eleven-year-old Ellie McDoodle illustrates her sketchbook with chronicles of her
adventures and mishaps while camping with her cousins, aunt, and uncle.
ISBN-13: 978-1-58234-745-5 • ISBN-10: 1-58234-745-X
[1. Camping—Fiction. 2. Cousins—Fiction. 3. Interpersonal relations—Fiction.
4. Adventure and adventurers—Fiction.] I. Title. II. Title: Ellie McDoodle.
III. Title: Have pen will travel.
PZ7.B28047El 2007   [Fic]—dc22   2006028424

First U.S. Edition 2007

Printed in the U.S.A. by Quebecor World Fairfield
2 4 6 8 10 9 7 5 3 1

All papers used by Bloomsbury U.S.A. are natural, recyclable products
made from wood grown in well-managed forests. The manufacturing processes
conform to the environmental regulations of the country of origin.

WARNING:

This spy sketchbook belongs to me,
Ellie* Marie McDoodle.**

DO NOT READ UNDER PENALTY OF PLAGUE & PESTILENCE!

—— No Mercy ——

* Eleanor. What can I say? My parents have bad taste in girls' names. Bad names should be illegal!

** It's really McDougal, but the kids at school call me McDoodle because that's what I love to do: draw.

Day 1 ← Wait, that is so stupid—Day 1 would be 100 million years ago when time began and it would mean nothing happened before . . . but PLENTY has happened.

THIS is the usual me.

Detail:

x-treme happiness

This is my parents racing to the airport because Dad's old uncle Peter died.

My family:

Dad and Mom are sad but happy. They get to travel and see old friends.

Risa, 17, and Josh, 14, are happy. They get to stay home without parents. Ben-Ben, 3, is happy because that's his only mood.

Why am I unhappy?

On the way to the airport, Mom and Dad dump Ben-Ben and me at our cousins' house.
Total dread for three reasons:
1. All of the cousins are pains.

Deanna, age 11   Eric, ← her twin   Tiffie, age 7

I really, really, REALLY can't stand Eric.

2.
Aunt Mug
and Uncle
Ewing are
pains, too.

She spits
when she yells.

His neck
turns red
when he's mad.

3. Ben-Ben is a monkey boy.

He never walks, only runs and climbs and crashes into everything. So he always wears a crash helmet. He ransacks my stuff.

As if that isn't bad enough, we're all going camping. With them, it's more like cramping.

My parents think this will be fun for me. They are of course delusional.

You love camping,
so this will be great!
See you in a week!
Take care of Ben-Ben!

So now I'm trapped in a steel projectile, hurtling down the highway into the Great Unknown with a bunch of control freaks and snotty-nosed brats. Eric started a fight with Deanna and Tiffie so Aunt Mug is making me sit next to him.

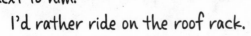

I'd rather ride on the roof rack.

Our Van

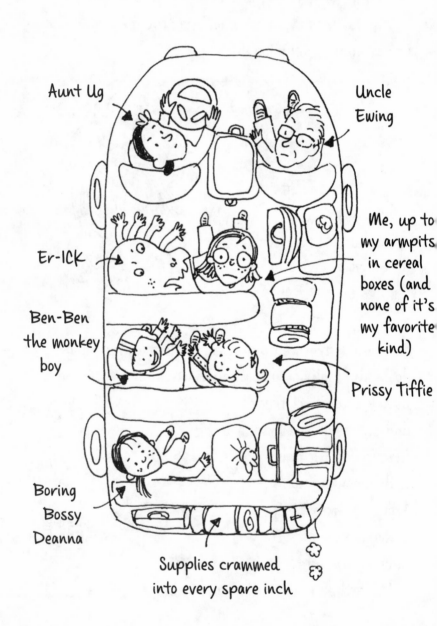

Aunt Ug

Uncle Ewing

Er-ICK

Me, up to my armpits in cereal boxes (and none of it's my favorite kind)

Ben-Ben the monkey boy

Prissy Tiffie

Boring Bossy Deanna

Supplies crammed into every spare inch

Why I have this sketchbook

1. To spy. No—OBSERVE things. I'm just observing life around me. Like in science class!
2. To remember important stuff.
3. Evidence of how demented this group is.
4. It's my only hope for keeping my sanity.

My view of the nearest window:

The History of Aunt Ug

Perpetual bad mood, and science has not yet determined WHY. Her name is actually Mug, not Ug. And I would NEVER call her Aunt Ug to her face.

When she was born, my mom couldn't say Margaret, so she called her Mug and the name stuck.

I would hate to have my sister name me. She has worse ideas than my mom.

Aunt Mug

as a baby

as a kid

as a teenager

as a bride

I think she smiled once but people were so shocked they forgot to take a picture of it.

CHARACTER STUDY
Uncle Ewing, the uncle

drawn by
Ellie McDoodle
Artist
Extraordinaire

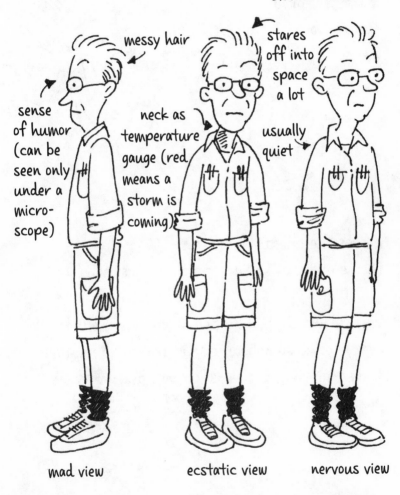

messy hair

stares off into space a lot

sense of humor (can be seen only under a micro-scope)

neck as temperature gauge (red means a storm is coming)

usually quiet

mad view   ecstatic view   nervous view

What does he like? I have no idea. I bet HE doesn't know, either!

As for Er-ick,
all I can say is that
ten minutes with him
makes my brain
scream for
mercy.

He lies, he cheats, he steals.
(Some of this I know for a fact, firsthand.)

When Aunt Ug buys a bag of cookies, he licks
every cookie so nobody else will want them. He is
a nose-picking, booger-slurping, bug-infested
parasite.

9

I'm saved by Aunt Ug, who FINALLY decides it's SNACK TIME.

> Take one bag and pass the rest back.

So of course Er-ick tries to take TWO bags.

Three cookies and a bunch of pretzel sticks.

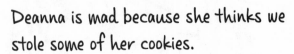

Now we're gonna be thirsty and they don't allow drinks in their van.

Deanna is mad because she thinks we stole some of her cookies.

Tiffie is whining because her bag dropped and the cookies broke.

It gets so noisy that Aunt Ug
starts a quiet contest.

What are you drawing?

SHHH!

Why?

Because it's a
quiet contest!

Is that my mom?
Did you draw my mom?

SHHH!

Is that my m—

SHHH!
Look, I'll give you
one of my cookies
if you'll be quiet.

Okay!
Also two pretzels!

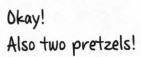

What's the point of a quiet contest? There's no prize. But it's better than hearing everyone fight, I guess.

Still, it's hardly quiet.

Quiet!
Be quiet!
It's a
QUIET
CONTEST!
Starting
RIGHT NOW!
Keep your hands
to yourself!
Eric!
Turn around!
Face the front!
Deanna,
DON'T MAKE ME
COME BACK THERE!!!

The aforementioned spit, and I am sitting too close. ARRGH!!!

What she really means: Don't make me come back there and spit on you!

Tiffie won the quiet contest, but there's no prize.
So she's sulking.

Cheezers. Get over it, Tiffie.
She's named after a fancy lamp, but this Tiffany
isn't too bright.

Understanding Tiffie:

very pretty

very empty

fancy hair

fancy clothes

fancy shoes

If Tiffie were a dog
she'd be a prissy little
frou-frou show dog
all fluffed up and barky.

Yap! Yap!
Yap! Yap!
Yap! Yap!
STOP IT!!

STUFF TO DO IN THE CAR

Read

Sketch

Sleep

SPY on the enemy

Observe (it's starting to rain)

Plan time AWAY FROM these people at camp

Write notes in disappearing ink*

* I love spy supplies

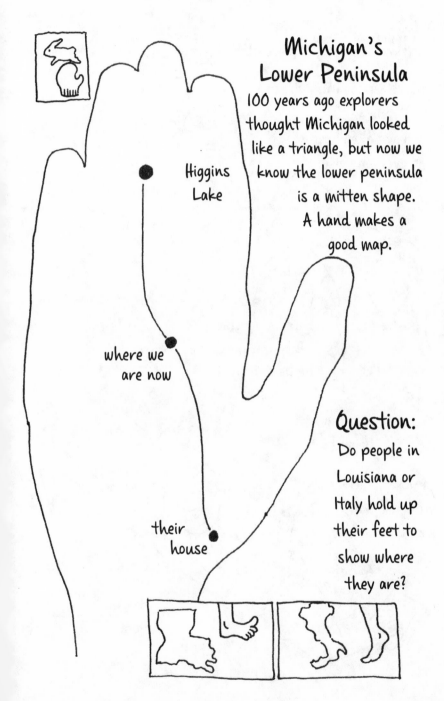

Michigan's Lower Peninsula

100 years ago explorers thought Michigan looked like a triangle, but now we know the lower peninsula is a mitten shape. A hand makes a good map.

Higgins Lake

where we are now

their house

Question:

Do people in Louisiana or Italy hold up their feet to show where they are?

Ahh, finally—LUNCH

It's pouring rain. Tiffie and I race ahead of everyone else.

Pick a good table

Aunt Ug

Uncle Ewing makes everyone be quiet at the table.

Deanna being boring

Er-ick the icky is eating all the sugar packets

Me (spying) next to Tiffie

Feed the jukebox

I choose "High Hopes"—Dad's favorite song, where the ant keeps trying & finally succeeds.

Tiffie chooses "The Hokey Pokey"—Grandpa's favorite.

Me Tiffie

I teach Tiffie how to draw ants on the napkins.

We both hold our pens weird, but not the same weird.

We draw faces on our hands and act out the Hokey Pokey.

"You put your right foot in . . ."

Tiffie wants me to write out all of the "High Hopes" song lyrics so she can memorize them.

Ben-Ben the crazy monkey boy runs all over the place

I wish I was home. These people are SO annoying.

Bleah.

17

Back in the car, and it's still raining.

I like to watch the little rivers of raindrops on the van windows and try to guess which direction they'll go. It's like they're alive.

I feel bad when they hit the window's edge. It's like they die.

Weird how you can just cross an imaginary line and the rain STOPS.   ☺

Er-ick is reading a graphic novel.
Interesting. I didn't think he could read.

You can tell you're getting close to camp by:
1. the hills on the highway
2. lots of forests
3. deer, back in the trees
4. touristy billboards

The Mystery Spot!
Mysterious!
(?) ←
North on I-75,
Exit at the big tree,
turn left at the fence

Souvenirs!
Flotsam & Jetsam
Castle of Trinkets
Every souvenir you can
imagine—and some you can't!

Fred Moose
Museum
It'll amaze and
a-moose you

I am an expert at camping. We always use tents and we've been coming to Higgins Lake since I was a baby, I guess, so I know the area really well.

These people hardly ever go camping and they're using a cabin.

Boring!

They wouldn't let me bring my own tent.

Tiffie has to go to the bathroom, and they're telling her to hold it because we're almost there and nobody wants to stop. We cross over the Au Sable River (pronounced "sahbo," NOT "saybul" like Deanna just said). Grandpa took me fishing on the Au Sable when I was four. (Tiffie's turning red.) Past the bait shop and the museum and the fish hatchery sign. (Tiffie's turning green.) FINALLY! State Park entrance. (Tiffie's eyeballs are yellow.) Check-in takes a longgggg time. At last we drive to the cabin. But Tiffie still has to run to the bathroom, six campsites away. She makes it. I go with her and tease her about ME taking the first available stall and making her wait. She cries over the dumbest things.

Cheezers.

Unpack. Assigned beds (of course).
It's a pretty small place.

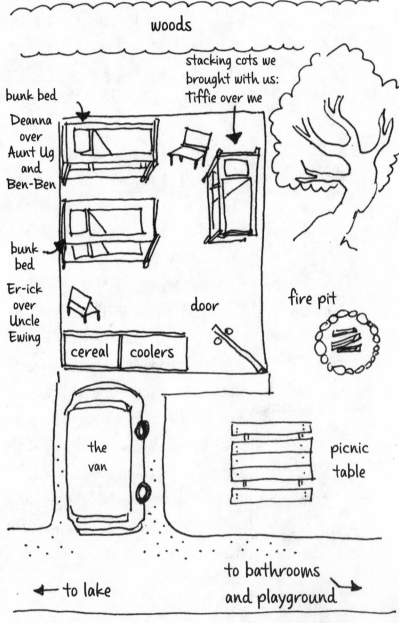

woods

bunk bed

Deanna over Aunt Ug and Ben-Ben

stacking cots we brought with us: Tiffie over me

bunk bed

Er-ick over Uncle Ewing

cereal

coolers

door

fire pit

the van

picnic table

← to lake

to bathrooms and playground →

Free time until dinner, but we have to stay near the cabin.

this book →

Boy, Tiffie sure cries easily.

It's rotten of you to tease her.

Huh?

Picking on a little kid. I expect more of you.

Deanna

CHEEZERS.

If I want to get reprimanded I'll hang out with Uncle Ewing. So I LEAVE. Yell at an empty swing, Duh-anna.

Grrrrr . . .

Deanna acts like she's SO smart, like she's really mature. But she is 4 months and 17 days YOUNGER than me.

And besides, she isn't that nice either. She pulls all the heads off Tiffie's dolls and puts their clothes on backward. You call that MATURE?

Anyway, I was just playing around.

I'm outta here.

HIGGINS LAKE CAMP

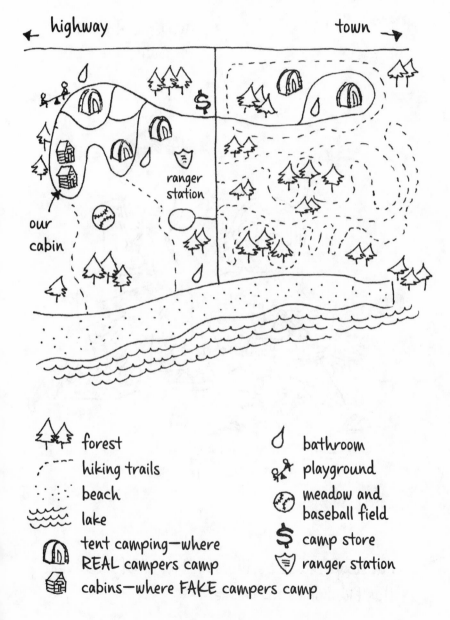

← highway   town →

ranger
station

our
cabin

🌲 forest
--- hiking trails
∴ beach
〰 lake
⛺ tent camping—where
REAL campers camp
🏚 cabins—where FAKE campers camp

◊ bathroom
🛝 playground
⚾ meadow and
baseball field
$ camp store
🛡 ranger station

I'm supposed to be the spy, but all of a sudden
this kid sneaks up on me.

This is Scott from Kalamazoo.

age: just turned 13

big, soft eyes

speaks French, Japanese, and English

wears a little pouch—I'm not sure what's in it

says he can't draw but wants to learn

medic kit in pocket

camouflage pants

Scott is mysterious. I think a person could talk to him for eons and still not know everything about him.

Scott and I take a walk in the meadow and the woods. We see deer! We're very quiet and one comes within 10 feet of us. Amazing!

tree swallow—blue-green shiny bird dives and glides gracefully

honey locust tree seed pod, eaten by deer, chipmunks, and squirrels

deer trail

blue racer snake, about 3 feet long

I can't believe how much
Scott knows about nature.

The coolest things we find:

Deer bones!
They're completely
white—Scott says
that means they've
been here a while.

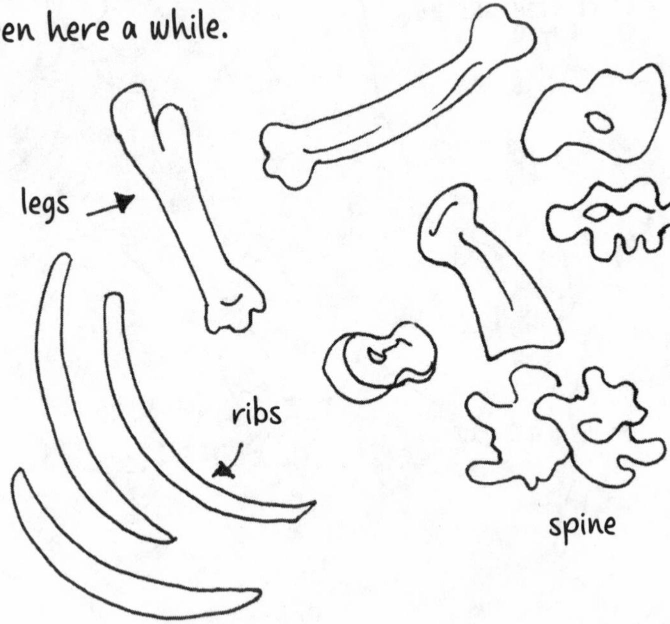

legs →

ribs

spine

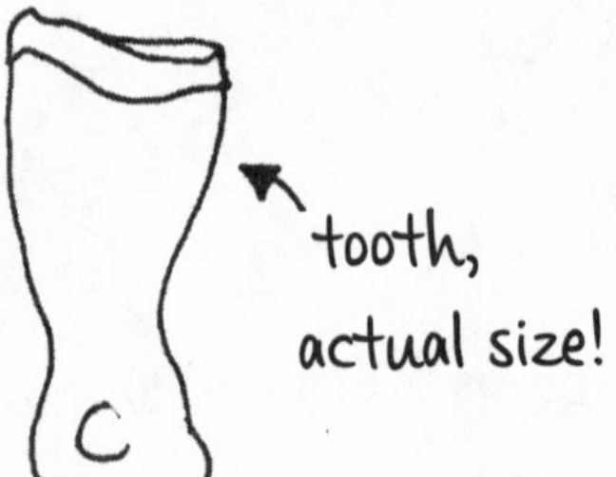

tooth,
actual size!

We're reassembling
the skeleton. It's
like a puzzle.
This is SO COOL!

Until Deanna finds us . . .

"Oh my GOSH! You guys are SICK! Those bones are DISGUSTING! And anyway you're in trouble, Ellie. You're late for dinner, PLUS you were supposed to stay within six campsites of our cabin."

Bye, Scott! See you after dinner!

Scott's Campsite is #137.

DINNER:
Hot dogs & chili &
baked potatoes

Aunt Mug isn't a bad cook, but I want to cook my own hot dog on a stick over the fire. Predictably, they say NO.

They also say I can't go visit Scott after dinner. Er-ick keeps trying to grab this book so finally I just have to sit on it.

Eric!
No more
potato chips.

There's
none left.
..

The girls do the dishes (boys will do breakfast).
Yippee. More time with Deanna.

She's as much of a control freak as her parents!
I get even, though.

So then I splash
her, but not very much,
and she slaps me with a wet
towel, which HURTS. Pretty soon we're both
being punished by: 1) having to do the dishes in
the morning, and 2) having to sit across from
each other for half an hour WITHOUT being mean
to each other.

I guess our grandpa used to stop fights this way
when our moms were kids. It's better than his
infamous Doorknob Punishment. (Hold your nose
against a doorknob until you're in a better mood.)

Also I wasn't allowed to work on this book for
half an hour.

Eventually I ask Deanna if she wants to play
20 Questions and she says yeah, so we do.

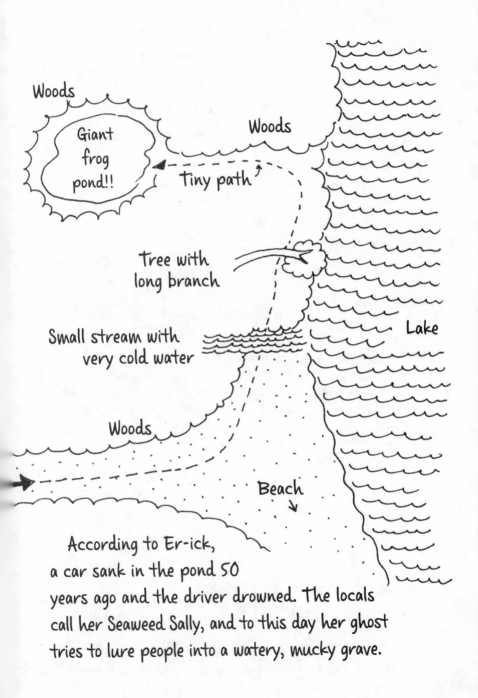

Woods

Giant
frog
pond!!

Woods

Tiny path

Tree with
long branch

Small stream with
very cold water

Lake

Woods

Beach

According to Er-ick,
a car sank in the pond 50
years ago and the driver drowned. The locals
call her Seaweed Sally, and to this day her ghost
tries to lure people into a watery, mucky grave.

Thick, deep, dark,
scummy pond.
I don't see a car or
any dead people.

Wow, Er-ick is right. I have
NEVER seen so many FROGS.
I'm drawing them (and looking at their ears)
but everyone else is catching them. I am morally
superior. Frogs don't belong in baskets and pails.

Big fat
bullfrogs, cute
little tadpoles,
teeny-tiny frogs.
They catch
DOZENS.

Of course, Aunt Ug won't let them bring the frogs inside the cabin. So they line up all the containers outside and cover the openings so the frogs can breathe but they can't escape.

So, what are you guys going to do with all those frogs?

Take 'em home as pets. Hopefully THIS time, some of them will survive.

Eventually we say good night to the frogs and go inside the cabin.

Geez. Why can't I use one tiny flashlight to work on my book?

My flashlight won't wake anyone up. His YELLING does, though.

I give up.

Good night.

Day 2

It's morning and it's raining outside. Bleah. This is torture. Wall-to-wall relatives. After three Quiet Contests, a half hour of forced reading (weird how being forced to do something you love makes you not like it), and a breakfast of their favorite cereal but not mine, I just want OUT.

Me: Can't I go out for a walk? I have a poncho.
Them: NO.

Aunt Ug passed out pipe cleaners and told us to make things we saw at camp. I made these:

I know who that is! It's that weird guy with the purse that Smellie was talking to!

I'm Er-ick and I'm a dotty mandrill!*

*crazy baboon

Then I get a genius idea. I teach them how to play Spoons. Er-ick wins without even cheating. This is actually fun but you won't catch me admitting that to anyone here.

HOW TO PLAY 🥄🥄 (SPOONS)

It's like musical 🪑s, but with 🥄s.

Deal each 🧍 4 🃏.

Dealer grabs 1 🃏 from the pile,

tries to match it with the 🃏 in his ✋,

and passes 1 🃏 to the player on his right.

Whoever has 4 of a kind first grabs a 🥄 quietly.

When the others notice a 🥄 is gone,

they try to grab a 🥄 also.

But with 5 🧍🧍🧍🧍🧍 you play with 4 🥄🥄🥄🥄,

so someone loses. The loser gets an "S."

Then start another round. If the same 🧍 loses again he or she gets a "P" until it spells out "SPOONS" and the game ends. (Each time you play a round, a new 🧍 gets to deal the 🃏.)

And if you have a 😀 like Ben-Ben around, it's good to give him extra 🃏 so he doesn't wreck your game.

After nine rounds of Spoons, things start to get ugly again so Aunt Ug and Uncle Ewing make us go to the . . .

FRED MOOSE
MUSEUM

This is good. I can go off on my own. Lots of
tourists here but I will spy on the dead animals
instead.

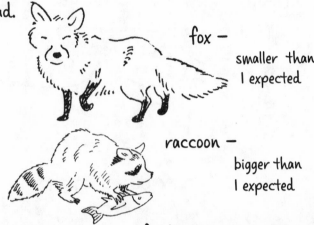

fox —

smaller than
I expected

raccoon —

bigger than
I expected

field mouse —

Once we caught a tiny field mouse in a big box,
in my dad's office. We left it for five minutes
to get a better cage and when we got back the
mouse had disappeared.

porcupine —

What's his favorite game?
Poker.

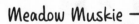

Meadow Muskie —

Fred Moose is
famous for this fish. Now extinct, it ran
on land with footprints facing opposite
directions, to fool its enemies. I was 10
before I realized it was a joke.

duck
(wood)

duck
(mallard)

goose
(Canada)

bald eagle
from 1857

Bald eagles aren't bald, except on their feet.

Native American
eagle symbol

Native American symbol
for stupidity

Eagles taste like chicken! Ha ha ha!

The Fred Moose people take their moose seriously.

The drinking fountain is a moose head.

All the people here are wearing moose souvenirs and giving the Fred Moose antler greeting.
I think it's goofy.

BEN-BEN
The Monkey Boy, Unleashed

Ben-Ben gets into everything as soon as you turn your back.

And he's always missing a sock and a shoe.

Totem pole goes up to the third floor

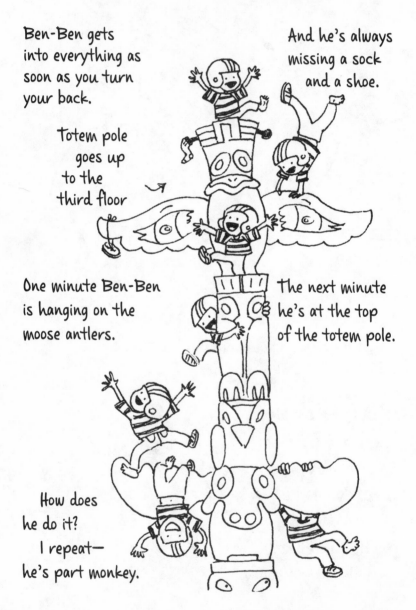

One minute Ben-Ben is hanging on the moose antlers.

The next minute he's at the top of the totem pole.

How does he do it? I repeat— he's part monkey.

A Study of Nearby Wildlife
Deanna, age 11.

dangerous talons

acute vision but not a cute face

highly vocal:
- shrill nasal bleats
- roars when angry
- aggressive growl
- barks out orders
- whimpers when she doesn't get her way

good at one thing: sports; gallops at moderate speeds.

Sometimes born in pairs: This specimen is the older of the twins by 3 minutes, and also is taller and dominant. This makes Er-ick feel unimportant, so he misbehaves.

Deanna, → dominant twin

Er-ick, inferior twin

Spying on people in the store . . .

Aunt Ug's trying to convince the younger kids they want cheap souvenirs instead of expensive ones. Tiffie gets a water bottle.

Er-ick spends his money on fake dog poop and plastic flies and of course candy.

Deanna buys a sweatband (ew) but what she really wants is the soccer ball.

Hey, Deanna! If you love it that much, why don't you marry it?

Oh, Er-ick, you are SO witty. My answers:
- Nah, he's too much of an airhead.
- He's a very well-rounded guy.
- They'd have a ball together.
- Let the good times roll!
- What would a love triangle look like?
- A year later they could have a bouncing baby boy.

Ben-Ben
was here

Uncle Ewing gets a book on astronomy.
I buy a bag of cool rocks and two books: *Survival*
and *Animal Tracks*.

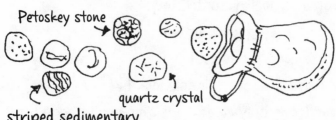

Petoskey stone

quartz crystal

striped sedimentary

Outside there's a double rainbow over the town.

Back at camp . . .

While Tiffie and Ben-Ben count worms on the ground by the cabin, I'm off to show Scott the sketches I did.

I let Scott read this book. His campsite feels more like what I'm used to. It's REAL camping. I'm embarrassed to be staying in the cabin with my cousins. It's too much like a hotel. I like roughing it instead.

Scott shows me what he keeps in his bag.

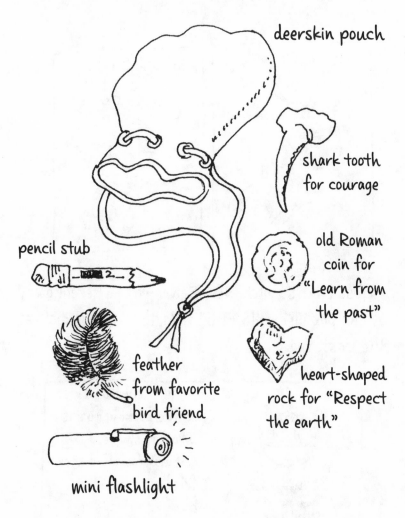

deerskin pouch

shark tooth for courage

pencil stub

old Roman coin for "Learn from the past"

feather from favorite bird friend

heart-shaped rock for "Respect the earth"

mini flashlight

We walk to the lake. It's too cold to swim, but we wade on the shore.

I can tell Scott almost anything, but I don't think I can tell him that I like him.

Dinnertime back at the cabin.

Yes. That's right. Ben-Ben is eating cereal out of the box WITH HIS FEET. It's the cereal I dislike the least, too.

All the wood is wet so the cooking fire is a pillar of smoke.
Smoky canned stew filled with ash from burning newspapers. YUM.

 Plus Er-ick puts plastic flies in everyone's food.

YIKES!

Must stay calm. Every move calculated.

I can't let them get curious about my book. They might gang up on me and try to steal it. Must keep this book out of enemy hands! Quick—divert their attention with a game.

Whew. Crisis averted. We play I Spy for a while
(until everyone just keeps guessing "a tree")
and then I get them to play Human Pretzel with
a bunch of other kids at the playground.

Hold on, and untangle into a big circle without letting go.

We play this four times, and each time Scott grabs my hand.

We do Fing Fang Fooey to figure out who will be "it" for the next game.

FING FANG FOOEY:
1. Everyone puts one hand in the circle.

2. Everyone says "Fing, Fang, Fooey!" while pumping their hand into the circle, and on the word "Fooey" everyone holds out 1, 2, or 3 fingers.

3. Add up all the fingers, then count around the circle starting with the youngest player. The player the number lands on becomes "it."

BLOB TAG:

"H" tries to tag someone.

When she does, they link arms & try to tag people.

Pretty soon "it" has turned into a huge blob.

It gets late and we go back to the cabin for a nice smoky campfire. Bleah.

Thanks to the rain, there are a million mosquitoes.

Double bleah.

And a zillion biting black flies. OUCH!

I go into the cabin early so I can work on my book. And when everyone else comes in to go to bed, they let in all the mosquitoes.

Ah, what a nice night.

:(

Day 3

ARRGHHH!

Tiffany PEED on me!!!

These stupid cots LEAK!!

And then—while carrying my stinking sleeping bag outside to air it out—I see a note!

What a find!

to Eric from ?

What a FAKE! Er-ick planted it for me.

Smelly Ellie You're a LOSER Hahaha

And now Aunt Ug's saying we have to go to the trout hatchery in town. I'm so sick of these people.

Uncle Ewing drops us off at the trout
hatchery while he goes to the laundromat.
Who has the tougher job? ME, I believe.

THE TROUT HATCHERY:

Stand around for hours and watch
fish swim. For excitement, pay 25¢
for a handful of fish food pellets to
throw into the water.

Er-ick puts
a handful of fish food down my
shirt, so now my back smells like
rotting skunky fish.

Somehow, some way, I will get revenge. I'll ask
Scott for some ideas on how to get even with Er-ick.

sand in his
sleeping bag

nest of spiders in his
duffel bag

Revenge, sweet revenge . . .

embarrass him

Eric likes to play
with dolls.

meat in his shoes

"Please, please, Ellie, I beg of you,
don't punish me anymore. I've
learned my lesson. I'll do whatever
you want from now on. Let me
do your chores."

Back at camp, FINALLY, with a clean sleeping bag that Uncle Ewing washed. It's the least he could do. I'm off to site #137 to find my only friend at this lousy campground . . . ☺

Oh, NO NO NO NO NO!

tent was here

tire tracks

Scott's family is GONE!

Now I'm really alone. Maybe I'll stay here all night. Just me and the bugs.

I just can't believe Scott left without saying good-bye. I can't believe I'm stuck with these awful relatives who wet their beds and micromanage my time.

My choices:

___ Tolerate them for 4 more days.

___ Hide until it's time to go home.

___ Be straight with them and tell them I can't stand them (start a WAR).

___ Take the bus back to my house.

___ Tell a park ranger I'm lost and need to get back home by tomorrow.

___ Form an alliance with one of them so at least someone is on my side.

Prediction for the rest of this camping trip:

okay___ bad___ awful___ terrible___
horrible___ worst ever___ disaster___

Maybe Scott left a message for me somewhere. This will take some detective work.

I am soooooo relieved. Even if I don't ever call him, it's nice to know that Scott left a good-bye message for me.

I decide to leave a tribute for him. He won't ever see it, but the earth knows it's there.

The elephant symbolizes wisdom, strength, good luck, and of course, never forgetting.

This is not good.
We are eating tacos for dinner, and nobody notices when Ben-Ben leaves the table.

Until he comes back,

holding
a frog—
the BEST frog—

way too tight.

Its guts are
oozing out.

I think this might be the very grossest thing I have seen in my whole life. And Ben-Ben has no idea what he did.

Uncle Ewing buries it. We make sure the rest of the frogs are okay. Aunt Ug puts dinner away and makes us get ready for a nature walk.

After the lake, we all go to the playground.
This part shocks me: They play tag! Mostly I
just take notes.

Tiffie gets
Ben-Ben or
Aunt Ug

Aunt Ug
gets Tiffie

Deanna
always
lets Ben-
Ben get her

Er-ick
mostly
chooses his
dad or the
younger kids
or me.

I'm surprised they are capable of playing a game together. Usually the only thing they do together is fight. Or imprison and kill frogs.

My new survival book tells how to get through hurricanes, quicksand, and tiger attacks, but it doesn't really help with my situation.

TIPS FOR SURVIVING CAMP
with relatives you can't stand

keep your distance

don't say much

don't pick up any of their bad habits

if confronted by the enemy, back away slowly

keep your eye on the prize

have a pen handy

They're done playing tag at the playground.

Hey—I have an idea! Lets go back to the cabin and play Hunka Bunka!

Huh?

What's Hunka Bunka?

It's where you play tag, but around the edges of a room. You're not allowed to touch the ground. You have to jump on the beds and dressers and stuff, and when you get to the door, you stand on the doorknob and swing to the other wall.

No, let's go see some stars instead.

I knew they wouldn't let us play it. I just wanted to give them ideas for more creative games than just tag.

Is that Orion?
No—he's in the winter sky.
Wait— DAD knows the stars??
Sure! I studied astronomy in college.
I see the Big Dipper!
Where's the Little Dipper?
Right there! See it?
Wowww.
I see Sirius!
Oh, be serious! Hahaha!
That star is Rigel.
That one is Castor, and there's Pollux.
I see the Milky Way.
I'm hungry!
Amazing how many stars you can see out here in the country.
Star light, star bright, first thousand stars I see tonight . . .
Twinkle twinkle little star . . .
Uh, I think Ben-Ben is eating a bug.

81

Day 4*

It's breakfast time and I'm already SICK of Er-ick.

He put stickers upside down by the bunk bed ladder.

Stickers.

Smellie ♥ purseboy

So of course I step all over them.

Not too bad, but when you need to run a half mile to the bathroom in the morning, seconds count.

And that's not all . . .

He ties my shoes together with tight knots.

And short-laces one side on each.

Plus he keeps trying to grab this book.

Aunt Ug says we all smell ripe and we have to take showers NOW. So, where to hide this book . . .

*Nobody peed on me overnight. Thank goodness.

IDEAS: Where to hide it

duct tape

No, no, no!!!
My duffel bag is the
FIRST place he'll look!

Ahh, nice shower. I come back to get my book and find this:

wet hair

My book is right where I left it.

NO FROGS!
Who would do this?
And did they see my book??
More important, did they read it?

I don't mind having Tiffie go with me. In fact, I think I prefer her company to everyone else's. Hey, maybe I can mold her into someone better!

These are rules for
life. Use them for
good and not for evil:

- Have courage.
- Learn from the past.
- Respect the earth.
- Play lots of games.
- Don't drink a lot of
liquids before bedtime.
- Don't worry so much
about what you look
like.
- Your family is strange.
Save yourself by not
getting too close to them.
- Always look for an exit
route.
- Remember the ant song.

Tiffie is a very good
student. She repeats
each point. And she
sings the ant song for
me. She memorized it
in just 3 days!
She reminds me of
myself at her age.

I showed her some stuff in the woods.

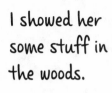

Poison ivy vines grow up trees

Poison ivy

if it has leaves of three, let it be

red stem where the leaves join it

Praying mantis

Females try to eat the males. They bite their heads off! Disgusting. But it's nice to see females get a-head sometimes.
ha ha

Bear tracks

same size as Tiffie's hand

Yikes! We have to be careful!

While Tiffie catches AND RELEASES frogs at the pond, I ponder the mystery of who emptied the frog containers.

Uncle Ewing
Aunt Ug
Deanna
Tiffie

> ? Maybe ?

Me
Er-ick
Ben-Ben

> No—
> didn't,
> wouldn't,
> or couldn't.

Whoever did it deserves an award because it SAVED all those frogs.

The Freedom Frog Award
For humanitarian and frogitarian services to our web-footed amphibian pals.

Oh, ICK.
Look who's here.

I just finished convincing Tiffie that it's bad to catch and keep frogs if you can't give them a good home, and here's Er-ick. He must have seen that the frogs were set free.

Writing this later—
It all happened so fast.

And it only gets worse.

So I jab a bigger stick at him, and hit him in the face, and he yells and yanks on it and then . . .

I freak out. Anyone would!

And I swear I could feel something
pulling on my shoes.

It was
TERRIFYING.

Fear turns to rage: He pulled me in
on purpose, I know it!
Suddenly I WANT to push him nder
so Seaweed Sally can get him.

But I concentrate on getting
myself out. I'm pulling on the grass
with all my might, my arms are sore,
my fingers are almost bleeding from
grasping at anything . . .

Suddenly I feel myself getting
pushed onto the edge of the grass.
It's adrenaline, I'm sure. People get
bursts of superhuman strength
when they're pushed to their limits.

I am
superhuman!

Er-ick is throwing up on the grass (so am I). I pull his hat out for him. It's not too slimy, surprisingly. Tiffie is still all upset about Seaweed Sally.

Then Er-ick starts running. At first I don't know what's going on, and then it occurs to me: The LAKE! I run too.

Higgins Lake is freezing cold because of all the rain we've had.

And it's super clear and not very deep.

The waves come in, bringing in little fishes and bits of driftwood, and the waves go out, taking bits of pond scum.

We stay in the water a long time, coughing and snorting and wheezing. I try to get all the algae out of my hair and my clothes—impossible.

Finally we walk back to camp without talking.

Holy cow. HE helped me out? When I didn't have any more strength, I felt something boost me up onto the grass. That was HIM? Courage and generosity? In Er-ick? Is that possible?

Why did you help me get out?

DUH! I had no choice! You were in my way so I had to push you out first.

We still get punished. We have to go to the hospital and cough up some gunk for the doctors to study to make sure we don't have some horrid pond scum disease now. Bleah.

Even worse, Aunt Ug makes us promise to be nicer to each other and quit the name-calling.

I have to think about all this.

I take another shower—
my third today. I still
don't feel clean.

Late dinner: FISH.
And spinach that
looks like seaweed.
It's disgusting.
I can't eat.

After dinner we
have a campfire.
Er-ick is pretty
quiet, like me.

I'm sitting where most of the smoke will blow into my face. I know it's weird, but it feels better to be in the smoke, like it's burning all the pond germs and scum out of me.

Ugh.

No matter how many times I swish water in my mouth and spit it out, I can still taste that frog algae.

Later, in the cabin. . .

Uncle Ewing says ten minutes until lights out.

I know what I have to do:
I have to go back to the frog pond.

It's like getting back up on a horse after it throws you.

I don't want to, though.

Day 5

I dream a bunch of frogs are holding me hostage until Er-ick promises not to capture any more of them. Which of course he won't promise. Then he morphs into a praying mantis and I wake up smiling.

While we are doing the breakfast dishes I ask Tiffie to go with me to see the frogs again.

By the time we're on the trail to the pond, everyone wants to go.

OPERATION POND RECONCILIATION

I am not afraid. I am not afraid.

my mantra

It's like a detective show. We locate
the log Er-ick fell off of, and the
sticks I used to try to save him, and
our sunken footprints and handprints
in the muck.

It's just a pond. Not very big. Maybe
not even very deep. I survived it and
I'm not afraid of it anymore.

I catch a frog, pet it, and let it go
in the swampy water.

Suddenly I know how it must
taste to kiss a frog.

Handsome prince or not,
I think I would decline.

Ew!

We go to the lake and Tiffie says we should make a giant sand frog in honor of our pond adventure, so we do. And we tell every silly frog joke we could think of.

Q: How deep should we dig the frog?
A: Knee-deep, knee-deep!

Q: What is a frog's favorite food?
A: French flies!

Q: Why are frogs so happy?
A: Because they EAT whatever bugs them!

Q: What animal has more lives than a cat?
A: A frog! He croaks every night.

Q: What do you call a frog who crosses the road, jumps in a mud puddle, and crosses over the road again?
A: A dirty double-crosser!

⋀ this means sacrificial animal

Then we wade in the lake, gathering the best rocks and shells.

this book

Minnows
They're so cute!
They dart around your
feet. I catch a minnow
with my bare hands—
you have to be FAST.

We put the rocks and shells around the giant sand frog to protect him.

LUNCH

Leftovers:
- Tacos (from Dead Frog Night)
- Fish (from Pond Scum Night)
- Hot dogs (from Only Creeps Pick on Tiffie Night)

Er . . . I think I'll have a peanut butter sandwich instead.

After lunch, we get to swim!

Things I like to do at the beach:
• Walk on my hands in the water.
  • Bury my toes in the cold sand under the water.

• Get my legs all messy with sand, and then lift them up and watch the sand slide off.
• Keep really still so the minnows think I'm a rock and swim near me.

minnows

(actual size)

I also like to walk on my knees so the water is right below my chin, and see how far I can go before the water hits my mouth.

I like to pretend I'm the sole survivor of the *Titanic* and see how long I can float on my back (a long time, which is why I am the sole survivor).

I like to run in the deeper water—I like how hard it is to move my legs, and the sound of the water WHOOSHing as I stride through it.

supermodel on a photo shoot

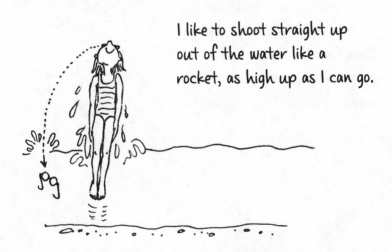

I like to shoot straight up out of the water like a rocket, as high up as I can go.

Mostly I like to be by myself at the beach (but not always).

I like getting buried in the sand and watching cracks form all over me as I slowwwly get up.

Yikes! Earthquake!

Sand castles are pretty good, giant frogs are better, and sand snowmen make people wonder if aliens have landed.

And this gives Deanna an idea . . .

PRANK

Deanna and I race back to camp to make a surprise for everyone else when they open the cabin door: two crazed camper dummies that we hope will make them scream like babies.

We shut the door and hide in the bushes across from the cabin. We have the perfect view, and we don't have to wait very long . . .

Ha ha ha ha ha ha ha ha ha ha ha ha ha ha ha ha

SUCCESS!

We laugh so hard our stomachs hurt.
They scream until they're hoarse. We have to give
them a chance to get over it (and maybe get even)
so we're going to rent bicycles for an hour from
the camp store.

Hiding this book at the end of my sleeping bag,
and we're outta here! (Still laughing, too!)

Who knew Deanna could be so creative?

No one likes
you, either.

OH MY GOSH OH MY GOSH OH MY GOSH!

While Deanna and I were out bike riding,
Er-ick found my book
and read it
and drew in it.

MY PRIVATE BOOK.

Could anything worse possibly happen?

No. This is just about as horrid as life gets.

Eric had this.
I believe it's yours.

this book

Me.
Run to the field.
NOW.

DAMAGE CONTROL:
Don't panic. THINK!

- How much did Er-ick read?
- Who else did he show MY BOOK to?
- Did Aunt Mug read it too?
- Can I live out here for 3 days?

YUM, DINNER!
Dandelion leaves are edible, and grasshoppers supposedly taste good compared to other bugs.

Yes, I will just live out here in the field eating bugs.

I can't BELIEVE he read my book. We were just starting to get along. He's a creep.

Things I could do:
1) Act like it never happened.
2) Tell them the whole book is just a joke.
3) Try to find out how much Er-ick read.
4) Take a bus home so I never have to face them again.

Oh, great. It gets even worse. Aunt Ug is headed this way.

Aunt Ug: Can we talk?

Me: Ulp. Uh. Yes?

Aunt Ug: I read your sketch diary.

Me: I was afraid of that.

Aunt Ug: You're very talented, Ellie.

Me: Huh?

Aunt Ug: You have a powerful voice and you're a natural leader. The other kids really look up to you.

Me: (blinking, this isn't what I expected to hear)

Aunt Ug: Did you know I was an artist when I was your age?

Me: You were??

She's nothing like an artist now.

Turns out Aunt Ug wanted to be a spy and an artist, but her parents thought she should be a secretary and then a wife and mom, so she gave up her dreams.

And you're not the first to call me Ug, either. Or to mention my spitting.

I feel my face turn red. I don't know what to say.

And then she says this:
   "You know, seeing you draw all weekend makes me want to get back into my art."
                    Wow.
My brain is in slow motion.
Aunt Mug as an artist?
No way. Well, maybe as a
grumpy, depressed one,
painting the *Moaning Lisa*.
Whistler's Mother would be *Spittler's Mother*. Ha!

Ellie, I know you haven't had an easy time with our family. But I appreciate that you've been a good influence on Tiffie.

Uh.

I think if you give the rest of us a chance, you'll find we're not your enemies.

You might even find we have something in common—like how you and I both like to draw. Speaking of which, maybe I will draw YOU sometime.

Draw me?

Sure. Artists only draw things they care about.

I finally get up the guts to ask her:
How much of my book did Eric read?

Probably all of it. He's a
fast reader. Plus it's an
interesting subject—HIMSELF.

Then she drops
the bombshell:

Ellie, I think you need to find Eric.
This is too big to ignore for three
days, and I don't like how you two
have been fighting all this week.

Okay.

Then she leaves.
This was a good talk at first. I'm not real happy
with how it ends.

I am a nice girl.
People like me at school.
I'm not rude to people usually.
I don't pull the wings off insects,
I don't hurt little kids on purpose,
I hold doors for old ladies.
I even apologize to chairs if I bump into them!
I don't steal things.
I don't wreck things.
In fact, I tried to save Eric's life!
I'm just normal.

SO WHY DO I
FEEL SO GUILTY?

Verdict: GUILTY!
Punishment: Operation Apology

1. Buy a candy bar at the
   camp store to use as bait.
2. Apologize to Er-ick the dung beetle
   (and he'd better apologize too).

I want to punch him in the mouth.

Okay, new tactic: Appeal to his sense of logic.

Look, you torpid sloth, if I were to let the frogs go, it would be on the last day so you couldn't go back and get more!

Speaking of which, you should be grateful because I saved your stupid hat!

For your information, it's a FEDORA, not a "hat." And YOU should be grateful I saved your stupid YOU!

Well, I AM!

So we agree! You're stupid!

This is so not going well.

Okay, deep breath. Trying again.

Er-ick, you could stop being such a pain and listen for once. I'm being nice and you're acting like a 3-year-old.

Oops. I must have hit a nerve. He explodes.

You think you're so smart, spying on everyone and acting like you're better than we are. You're a LOSER and a LIAR and you SMELL.

Great. So much for Operation Apology. All I did was make the warthog angry.

Ha! We have a little more in common than I thought.

FINALLY an agreement.

We lay out our arsenal and decide on a strategy: disappearing ink spitballs.

ERIC'S AUTOMATIC SPITBALL MACHINE USING A CHEAP MECHANICAL PENCIL:

① Unscrew tip and throw away.

② Pull eraser part out until it breaks loose.

③ Break off tip.

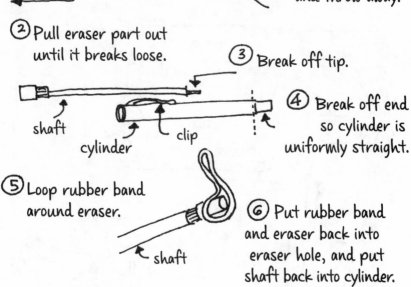

shaft

cylinder

clip

④ Break off end so cylinder is uniformly straight.

⑤ Loop rubber band around eraser.

shaft

⑥ Put rubber band and eraser back into eraser hole, and put shaft back into cylinder.

⑦ Loop other end of rubber band around clip, maybe twist it a few times.

⑧ To load it:

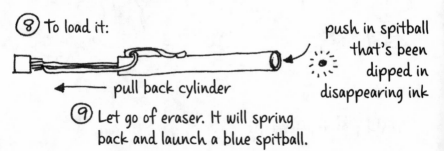

pull back cylinder

push in spitball that's been dipped in disappearing ink

⑨ Let go of eraser. It will spring back and launch a blue spitball.

I decide to quit drawing Eric as a monster, in an effort to get along.

Our plan works! Only one problem . . .

Deanna is a total snitch.

And Aunt Mug
still spits when
she yells.

They say:
- we're a bad influence on the other kids,
- disappearing ink doesn't always disappear from clothing,
- this is the stupidest stunt they ever saw,
- we have to do the dishes for the rest of the trip,
- no more pranks,
- any more fights or complaints and we're grounded to our bunks for the rest of the trip, and
- spitballs are disgusting and could be dangerous and there is zero tolerance for them.

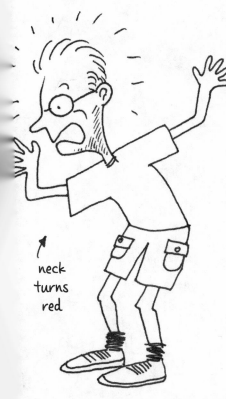

neck turns red

Yikes. Damage control time.

When they're done I stand up and repeat back to them what they just said (an old trick I learned from Risa and Josh). This technique always works. They realize I was listening and it prevents more lecturing.

At dinner I make a list with everyone. This is our last night at camp and we have to do something truly great.

- ☐ bear hunt (no way—I'll sing the bear hunt song, but I'm not hunting)
- ☐ play sardines
- ☐ nature walk (without parents)
- ☐ go to bed early
      Oh thank you so much for that
      suggestion, Aunt Mug!
- ☐ wash the van
      Another great suggestion, courtesy
      of Uncle Ewing.
      Maybe we should make this list
      where grown-ups can't hear us . . .
- ☐ get kids from other campsites together for a giant hide-and-seek game
- ☐ catch some frogs
          Uh, no.
- ☐ take Ben-Ben to the playground
      Be responsible for the monkey
      boy? NO WAY.
      We gotta get out of here FAST.

CHOOSING WHO IS "IT"

Say a rhyme while tapping each shoe around the circle. Whoever you land on last is out.

The last shoe left in the circle is "it" for the game.

Train, train, number 9, coming down Chicago line, if the train should jump the track, do you want your money back? Yes, no, or maybe so? Y-E-S spells yes and you are not "it!"

yes

Eric
Deanna
Tiffie
me

Bubble gum, bubble gum, in the dish, how many pieces do you wish?

5

One—two—three—four—five and you are not "it!"

My mother, your mother, live across the street. 18-19 Broadway Street. Every night they have a fight and this is what they say:
Acka backa soda cracker, acka backa boo. Acka backa soda cracker, out goes YOU!

I am "It."

We play SARDINES.

I LOVE this game.
It's like the
opposite of
hide and seek.

The person who
is "it" hides and
everyone else tries
to find him.

When you find him,
you quietly crawl
in and hide there too.

Pretty soon you have a whole bunch of
giggling friends all squeezed into
one little space.

The last person to find "it" loses the game
and the first person to find "it" is the new "it"
for the next game.

This is my best place to hide.
But Eric accidentally sits on Tiffie's head. Oops.

We decide to go on a nature hike. Our inventory:

Eric's Boy Scout knife	my mini first-aid kit	Deanna's watch
my book on survival in the wild	my compass	Deanna's granola bar and two dollars
my bandana	Ben-Ben's head lamp flashlight (he won't know— he's asleep)	Tiffie's water bottle on a belt
a box of cereal— snack-size Sugar Blaster O's	Deanna's sweatband	my book and pen
Eric's stash of candy, which we promise not to eat unless we get really desperate	my book of animal tracks	Eric's empty water balloons (8)
		8 eyes 8 ears 8 hands 8 feet

Eric wants to see a bear.
I'd prefer something less ferocious.

First order of business: A symbol for good luck on our path. 🐛

This is so cool. It's like we own the forest. The trees bow to our will.

A rabbit!

Bats!

We find a chipmunk that takes cereal right out of Eric's hand (but ONLY his).

Rabbits are too scared of us to even come near. Too bad—no cereal for them!

Tiffie's picking dandelions for Aunt Mug. We see:

daisies   black-eyed   Queen   Dandelions   Indian
             Susans   Anne's lace   blankets

We find a branch that bends over the path like a bench. It's very comfortable!

Wintergreen!
Shiny green leaves.
Tear a leaf and smell
it—it smells like gum!

about 4 inches

Diving to catch bugs. They ignore the cereal we throw.

Tie the tops of saplings together and throw a poncho over it to make a little house.

We could LIVE out here!

my bandana

Bad news: Fern stems rip your hand if you try to pick them. Tiffie finds out the hard way. OUCH!
Cold water from her water bottle helps.

To cheer her up we start singing camp songs.
Deanna starts this: Twinkle, twinkle, little star,
how we wonder where we are.
I add: We just want to find our way,
to our camp before it's day.
Eric wrecks it with: Twinkle, twinkle, take us home,
cuz this is a goofy poem.

 I'm hungry and we ate all the candy already.

Okay, fine. They're badger tracks. Good job making me feel stupid, Deanna.

Tiffie asked what we would do if it WAS a bear, and I pulled out my survival book:

Bears are most dangerous when they're hungry or with their cubs. If attacked, fall to the ground and roll into a ball, protecting your neck. Play dead. If a bear attacks you in your tent, fight back. Aim for the eyes and nose.

Take that, Deanna.

And for a mountain lion, you make a lot of noise and wave your jacket so you look bigger. Fight back aggressively, aiming for the eyes and mouth. Protect your neck and throat because that's how they kill their prey.

Eric: If I see a bear out here, I'm running.
Me: The book says not to! You can't outrun a bear!
Eric: I don't have to outrun the bear. I only have to outrun YOU. Ha ha ha ha!
Me: Grrrrr.
Tiffie: I'm thirsty and I'm out of water.
Me: Bite the tip of your tongue. That's an old Girl Scout trick.
Eric: Put a clean pebble in your mouth. Old Boy Scout trick.
Tiffie: Which one should I do?
Deanna: Pebble. Biting your tongue will hurt—duh!
Me: No! Bite your tongue! You don't bite it HARD. Duh!
Deanna: Two against one. We win. Right, Eric?

Deanna: Where IS Eric?

All roads lead to Rome, my dad always says.
Well, I hope not! We want HOME, not Rome. I
decide to make up a song:

> This is the path that never ends.
> Yes, it goes on and on, my friends.
> Some people started walking it
> Not knowing where it led
> And they'll continue walking it
> Forever 'til they're DEAD.
> This is the path that never ends . . .
> (repeats)

Guys, be quiet.

ERIC!

Hmm. I guess we should look for him.

We shout until our throats hurt. And we don't have any water.

Where is he?

My survival book is no help for this. I admit it—I'm getting worried.

This compass is useless, too.

It points in directions, sure. But we want it to point the way out of here.

← A more useful compass

What should we do? We can't go home without him.

Mom and Dad would kill us.

What if a bear got him?

Or Seaweed Sally?

I'm scared.

If we ever find him I'm going to be nice to him.

Do you think he's dead?

I don't know.

∴ Let's keep looking for him.

This next part happens fast.

Eric jumps out from behind a tree.

RAH!

Startled, Tiffie trips over a tree stump.

She cuts her shin.
         And twists her ankle.
                  Cheezers.
                  No water to clean it.
                  No extra bandana.
                  Deanna doesn't want her
                  precious sweatband to get
                  blood on it.

So I donate my sock as a bandage.

Yes, that's spit.

RULES:
1. No more separating from the group.
2. No more getting hurt.

My arms and back are aching.
Did I only carry her for 7 minutes?
It felt like 100.

Deanna's watch is handy. I only get to write in
this book when we rest, after 3 carries.

It's getting too dark to see,
and Eric's stingy with
the flashlight.
 Which, by the way,
 is growing dim.

Two more
minutes.

 8:45p.m.:
New problem:
We saw a big elk
and had to go off
the trail to get
around him. He's
chewing something.
Maybe his last victim.

Now we can't find the trail.

9:00 p.m.:
Deanna says we should plan to sleep out here.
I say that would be dangerous.
We're fighting over what's best.
My arms hurt.
Tiffie's crying.

9:20 p.m.:
We can't carry Tiffie 7 minutes. It's 5 minutes now,
then we switch. The flashlight's fading fast. Tiffie
put her bouquet inside her water bottle so she won't
have to carry it. She's a smart little kid.

Dad & Mom, I love you! ← just in case we don't make
it back

9:31 p.m.:
It's hard walking and carrying Tiffie.
Spiderwebs stretch across my face—creepy!
Sometimes I can feel something crawling on my
neck but can't scratch it because my arms
are full of Tiffie.

Witchy tree branches
pull at us,
ripping my
shirt. I have
a thousand
scratches
on me.

9:39 p.m.:
Deanna and Tiffie are yelling for help.
Maybe a ranger will hear us. Or at
least it'll keep the bears away.

I'm thirsty. My legs itch.
Flashlight's almost gone.

Are we gonna die out here?

If someone finds this book,
know that we tried our best.
Give my book collection
to Amy, my best friend.

Written later:
While carrying Tiffie I have an idea: We all stay super
quiet and see if we can identify any sounds or smells to
help us figure out where we are, or how to get out of
the woods. We hear crackling and owls and insect
sounds—but—
        WAHOO! We also hear frogs!
We follow the sound to THE POND!
    But it doesn't look like the pond we know, especially
in the moonlight.

But then Eric finds the symbol I put there earlier, made with sticks.

It means "Group desires a peaceful relation"— I put it there to apologize for the big dead bullfrog.

WHAT A RELIEF!!!

From the frog pond it's easy to get back to the cabin. Easier to see, too, because no trees block the moon. We run part of the way.

10:00 p.m.:
Aunt Mug starts crying when we walk into camp.
Uncle Ewing looks stunned (kind of, it's hard to tell
with him).
The rangers look happy at least.

↑
Aunt Mug looks like
she just rode a
merry-go-round
upside down.

. Aunt Mug and
Uncle Ewing read my book
(just the woods adventure)
and they let us stay up at
the campfire for a while.

After an ice pack on
her ankle, burn cream on
her hand, and bandages
for her cuts, Tiffie will be
okay.

Now that we're safe
and warm with snacks,
we're thinking this was a
pretty cool last night at
camp. We can't stop
talking about it.

We made it out of the
woods because we all
worked together. But I
wasn't REALLY scared.

Well, maybe a little.

Maybe I can help . . .

THE NEWT STORY

I tell them about my mom and Aunt Mug's two newts. I've heard the story a hundred times.

They kept them in a giant pickle jar.

One time they discovered one of the newts was super fat.

floating rocks

pump

aerator ball

tube

It turned out the aerator ball had come off the tube, so the tube sent a lot of big air bubbles into the water and the newt swallowed them.

Grandpa had to rub the newt really carefully so it could burp out all the air.

Aunt Mug laughs (that's a very good sign).

Day 6

It's freezing outside, which makes it easier to accept that we're ending camp today.

Still, I don't want to go home. Ha! I never thought I'd feel that way.

(annoyed)

Funny how last night was so miserable but now we're having fun talking about it.

We have a ton of stuff to pack up.

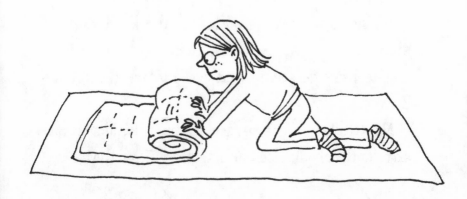

Load the van.
Clean the cabin.
Get on the road
after lunch.

Good-bye, Higgins Lake! I'm sad to leave.

We played the Alphabet Game once we hit the highway.

To play:

On signs and license plates, find a word that starts with an A, then a B, then a C . . .

The first person to find every letter from A to Z wins.

No doubles: If one person finds an E, like on an exit sign, nobody else can use that E on that sign.

My family always plays the Alphabet Game on long car trips, and I always lose because I'm slower to see things. But with these guys, I have a fighting chance!

After the Alphabet Game, we play the Question Game. Hold a normal conversation, but everything has to be a question.

And it goes on and on . . .

We get to Aunt Mug's house in time for dinner (pizza, yum) and unpack the van and put everything away.

Mom and Dad are coming tomorrow at noon to get me. I'm kind of happy about that (I'll be able to call Scott) and kind of sad. I sort of felt like triplets with Eric and Deanna.

I'm thinking it might be cool to spend more ti—

Whoa!

WATER
BALLOONS!

This means **WAR!** Ben-Ben is pelting me with water balloons. Eric must have put him up to it! Quick—must hide the book.

Writing this later . . .

Eric and Ben-Ben have pails full of water balloons (COLD water, too), and sneak up on each of us girls.

BUT WE GET THEM BACK!

First we run inside. Of course they think we're tattling on them—but we are really putting this book out of the line of fire and filling Deanna's stash of water balloons.

SPLAT!!

We catch them completely off guard.

Garbage can lids for shields don't help them very much.

But Ben-Ben is the sneaky little stealth blaster, fearlessly running under the line of fire and splashing us with cups of water. Then he grabs the garden hose . . . I'm laughing so hard. We're all soaking wet by the time Aunt Mug calls us inside.

Deanna, Tiffie, and I sleep in the living room, like a slumber party.

I had a lot more fun with you guys than I thought I would.

Well, we had more fun with YOU than we thought we would!

Hmm. That doesn't sound like a compliment. But I'll ignore it. Good night. ☺
(I have 24 mosquito bites just on one ankle.)

Day 7

Aunt Mug takes us to an art store. I LOVE ART STORES!
She buys paints for herself. And sketchbooks!

For her, Tiffie, Eric, and ME.

She says there are two rules for my sketchbook:
1. Have fun with it.
2. If I ever have a problem, talk about it instead of keeping it to myself.

I think I can manage that.

Next we go to the pet store to get Eric and Deanna some newts.

They're soooo cute.
(the newts, I mean)

Back to Aunt Mug's house just in time . . .

Still, it's nice to go home.

So, what did you learn?

THINGS I'VE LEARNED

1) Things aren't always as they seem.
2) You can't judge a book by its cover, or a vacation by its first day, or the value of a camping trip by whether it's in a tent.
3) Eric isn't so bad, I guess.
4) The monkey boy is smarter and more fun than I thought. Actually, my cousins are too.
5) If things aren't working out, be patient. It'll change (just like Michigan weather).
6) Elk are not meat eaters but they're still awfully scary.
7) Carrying a 7-year-old through a pine forest is quite a big job.
8) Spying is cool, but you should expect to get caught.
9) No girl is an island. We're all in this together. Might as well try to get along.
10) Eating bugs is overrated.

Mom said there are more surprises coming this summer.

One thing's for sure: I'll need lots of sketchbooks!

DATE DUE			

**FIC
BAR**

**Barshaw, Ruth
McNally.**

**Ellie McDoodle :
have pen, will
travel**